Dragon Slayers' Academy™ 7

WHEEL OF MISFORTUNE

By Kate McMullan
Illustrated by Bill Basso

SCHOLASTIC INC.
New York Toronto London Auckland Sydney
Mexico City New Delhi Hong Kong Buenos Aires

For L. F. M.
—K. McM.

ISBN 0-439-85240-4

12 11 10 9 8 7 6 5 4 3 2 1   6 7 8 9 10 11/0

Printed in the U.S.A.   40

First Scholastic printing, April 2006

Chapter 1

"You three!" Frypot called, hurrying into the Dragon Slayers' Academy kitchen.

Wiglaf, Angus, and Erica looked up from the soapsuds in the kitchen sink. They had been in Scrubbing Class all afternoon, scouring greasy pots and pans.

"Us three?" they asked together.

"You are the only three here," Frypot pointed out. "Who else could I mean? Mordred wants to see you. Put down your scrub brushes—"

Three scrub brushes splashed into the suds.

"And get yourselves to Mordred's office," Frypot said. "On the double!"

The three raced out of the DSA kitchen.

"Angus," Wiglaf said as they ran, "what do you think your uncle Mordred wants?"

Angus shrugged. "Most likely he wants us to scrub the privy."

"Or clean out the henhouse," suggested Erica.

Wiglaf feared his friends were right. The headmaster of Dragon Slayers' Academy never sent for his students to give them good jobs. Maybe he had more scrubbing for them. Or maybe something worse.

Wiglaf wondered how Angus felt about his uncle Mordred never giving him a break on the chores. He also wondered what Erica thought of so much scrubbing. Nobody but Wiglaf knew that she was really Princess Erica, daughter of Queen Barb and King Ken. Erica longed to be a dragon slayer, so she disguised herself as a boy and went by the name of Eric. She fooled Mordred. He had let her into the all-boys DSA. Surely at home in the palace, Erica never had to scrub anything. Yet she never complained.

The three reached the headmaster's office. Angus knocked on the heavy wooden door.

"Enter!" cried Mordred.

They walked inside. Wiglaf was surprised to

see three stools lined up facing Mordred's big desk.

"Come in." Mordred waved them into his office. "Sit down."

They sat. Wiglaf saw that three small pots of ink had been placed on Mordred's desk. A writing quill lay across each pot.

What is Mordred up to? Wiglaf wondered.

"The three of you are always in that laboratory," Mordred began as he picked up some parchment sheets from his desk

"What laboratory, Uncle?" asked Angus.

"The one in the North Tower," Mordred said. "The one with all the books."

"Do you mean the library, sir?" Erica asked.

"Library, laboratory." Mordred shrugged. "My point is that you seem to like books. Perhaps you have even read one?"

"A good many of them, sir," Wiglaf said.

"Fine!" Mordred boomed. "For I have heard it said that reading can add to one's knowledge."

"That is true, sir," Erica told him. "I have read seven books about Sir Lancelot and—"

"Good, good. Now let's see what else you

know," Mordred cut in. He began handing out the parchment. "These are your answer sheets."

Wiglaf took a sheet. It had numbers on it and circles filled with tiny letters *a*, *b*, *c*, and *d*.

"Here are your test booklets," Mordred added. He put one on each desk. A blob of sealing wax kept the students from peeking inside.

"What test are we taking, sir?" Erica asked.

"Shhhh!" Mordred said. "No talking! This is the S.A.T.–M.E."

"What does that stand for, sir?" Wiglaf asked.

"Some Awful Test, Medieval Edition," Mordred answered. "It is an all-day test. But *I* haven't got all day. So work fast, lads. The test will tell me how smart you are."

"Why do you need to know that, Uncle?" Angus asked.

"No more questions!" Mordred said. "When I say 'begin,' begin. And make no mistakes," he added. "Erasers have not yet been invented. Ready?" Mordred's violet eyes swept from Wiglaf to Angus to Erica. "Begin!"

Wiglaf broke the sealing wax. He opened his test booklet to:

Section 1: Reading Comprehension

MOLD: OUR FUNGUS FRIEND

What is mold exactly? Scholars in Toenail tell us that mold starts out as dust from mouse droppings. Scholars in East Armpittsia argue that mold begins as droplets of troll sweat. Scholars in West Upchuckia say that mold comes from a hermit scratching his head. But on one thing these wise men all agree: Mold is our fortune-telling fungus friend.

Wiglaf wondered who had written this drivel.

White, fuzzy mold on your bread means you shall dance a jig at your cousin's wedding. Green mold warns you to stay away from beehives. Purple mold? Beware a bearded stranger pointing a great big knife at you and screaming, "Give me all your money!" If the mold on your bread oozes black slime, it's time to get yourself measured for a shroud.

Wiglaf's stomach lurched. Why, he had a blob of dark goo on his bread that very morning! This was more than Wiglaf cared to know about mold. Or the future. He decided to skip to the questions.

1. What is mold?

a) A paste we use to clean our teeth
b) A fungus
c) Yucky
d) A tasty topping for toast

Wiglaf circled *c*. He read the next question.

2. *Where is mold likely to be found?*
   a) In the kitchen
   b) On peasants
   c) On your bread
   d) Up people's noses

Wiglaf gagged. He went on to the next question.

3. *Does mold have any practical uses?*
   a) Yes, as a household cleaner
   b) No, not a single one
   c) Yes, as a ladies' perfume or aftershave
   d) We don't know. What do you think?

Wiglaf sighed. He wished he were back scrubbing boar grease out of the cauldron.

4. *What can we do to keep mold from forming?*

a) Keep it from forming? Why would
   we want to do that?
b) Jump up and down on one foot while
   shouting, "Die, fungus!"
c) Never store your bread in a swamp.
d) Sacrifice a live chicken.

"Stop!" Mordred cried.

"But, sir!" Erica said. "I am not finished!"

Mordred snatched up the answer sheets. "We are short on time here." He took out *The Headmaster's Answer Guide to the S.A.T–M.E.* He began checking their tests.

At last Mordred slammed the answer book shut. He eyed Wiglaf. "Nice work, lad. You only missed one."

Wiglaf smiled. He was not going to point out that he had answered only one question.

"You three will do!" Mordred exclaimed.

"Do for what, sir?" asked Wiglaf.

"For the team," Mordred replied. "You shall represent DSA in the All-Schools Brain-Power Tournament!"

"We shall make DSA proud, sir!" Erica said.

"That's the spirit, Eric!" said Mordred. "This is the first year DSA has been invited to the tournament. We will be competing against Dragon Stabbers' Prep, Knights R Us, and Knights Noble Conservatory. The winning school always gets hundreds of new boys applying." He rubbed his chin thoughtfully. "If you win, I could hike up the tuition. Maybe as high as nine or ten pennies a year."

"Is there a prize for the winning team, Uncle?" asked Angus.

"You ninny!" Mordred exclaimed. "Would I have gotten you out of Scrubbing Class if there were no prize? The prize," he added, as a golden glow lit his violet eyes, "is a huge gold trophy filled with one gold coin for every point scored by the winning team."

"Oh, boy!" cried Angus.

"The gold is for *me*," Mordred snapped. "Er... I mean, for dear old Dragon Slayers' Academy." Mordred turned toward the doorway. "Bragwort!" he bellowed. "Come here and meet your teammates!"

Chapter 2

ragwort?" Wiglaf turned to Erica. "Is not Bragwort the student who always reminds Sir Mort when he forgets to give us a test?"

Erica nodded. "That's him."

"I always get an A+ on all Sir Mort's tests," a boy said from the doorway of Mordred's office.

Wiglaf saw that it was Bragwort, all right. He was tall, with curly yellow hair. His turned-up nose reminded Wiglaf of his pet pig's snout.

"I do so well that Sir Mort lets *me* grade his test papers," Bragwort went on.

"No wonder you get an A+," Angus murmured.

"Bragwort did not miss a single question on his S.A.T.–M.E.," Mordred said.

"Naturally," Bragwort said. "I never do."

"So he shall be the team captain," Mordred added.

"No fair," Erica muttered.

Mordred didn't seem to hear her. He was beaming at Bragwort.

"Worry not, sir," Bragwort put in. "With me on the team, losing is impossible!"

"We must prepare," Erica said. "Let us go up to the library. Surely Brother Dave will have some excellent books to lend us."

"Sorry," said Mordred. "No time for that sort of thing. The teams must register at Knights Noble Conservatory tomorrow evening. You'll have to leave right away. I shall come to KNC on Saturday afternoon to take home the gold that you have won for me. Score high, lads! Now, be gone!"

"I'm already packed," Bragwort told his team-mates. "I'll meet you by the gatehouse."

Wiglaf, Erica, and Angus hurried to the Class I dorm room. Wiglaf quickly threw his things into his pack: his rusty sword, a change of underwear, and his least dirty socks. Then the three stopped by the DSA kitchen.

"Just in time to finish up before suppertime." Frypot said when he saw them. "There is still a layer of boar grease on the cauldron."

"Sorry, sir," said Wiglaf. "But we must journey through the Dark Forest this very night."

"Whatever for?" asked Frypot.

"Mordred has chosen us to represent DSA in the All-Schools Brain-Power Tournament at KNC," Erica said proudly.

"May we have some food to take along?" asked Angus. "And some for Bragwort, too, I suppose."

"And please, sir," Wiglaf added, "no lumpen pudding."

"What!" cried Frypot. "Insult my lumpen pudding, will you?"

"I did not mean to..." Wiglaf began.

"I make the best lumpen pudding this side of Camelot," Frypot muttered. "But it's not good enough for you picky eaters." He grumbled darkly to himself as he banged jars and flasks around.

"Nice going, Wiglaf," said Angus, who took matters of food quite seriously. "Now Frypot will fix us something awful."

At last Frypot handed them four packages wrapped in parchment. "Jellied eel with a side of eel fries," he said. "And for dessert..."

"Yes?" said Angus eagerly.

"Eel custard," Frypot said. "Baked it just last week." He frowned. "Or was it the week before?"

The DSA team made faces behind Frypot's back. But they took their food and hurried from the kitchen. They ran out into the castle yard. Daylight was fading fast.

As they headed for the gatehouse, Wiglaf heard a voice calling: "Iglaf-way! Ait-way!"

Wiglaf squinted into the dusk. He saw his pet pig, Daisy, trotting across the castle yard toward him. Daisy had traveled with Wiglaf from his father's cabbage farm in Pinwick. On the way, a wizard had put a speech spell on her. Now she could speak, but only in Pig Latin.

"Hello, Daisy old girl," Wiglaf said. "You have come just in time to see us off."

"Oing-gay ow-nay?" asked Daisy. "In-yay ee-thay ark-day?"

"Yes, we're going in the dark." Angus nodded. "We must be at KNC by tomorrow evening."

"Et-lay ee-may ome-cay ith-way oo-yay," Daisy suggested.

"Come with us?" Wiglaf said. "Oh, Daisy, I think not. For we are to match wits with other lads in a brain-power contest."

"I-yay an-cay ee-bay our-yay oach-cay," Daisy said.

"You? Be our coach?" said Angus.

"But what does a pig know about answering really, really hard questions?" Erica asked.

"Enty-play," said Daisy. "Other-bray Ave-day ings-bray ee-may ooks-bay om-fray ee-thay ibrary-lay. I-yay ead-ray all-yay ay-day."

Erica turned to Wiglaf. "Is this true?" she asked. "Does Brother Dave really bring her library books?"

Wiglaf nodded. "Daisy reads three or four books a day."

"Then perhaps she can help us," Erica said thoughtfully.

"She could quiz us as we walk," said Angus.

Wiglaf smiled. "We shall be glad of your company, Daisy," he said. "Let us be off."

They walked to the gatehouse.

"Took you long enough," Bragwort said when they reached him. "I, myself, am never late." He frowned at Daisy. "Be gone, swine!"

"This is my pet pig, Daisy," Wiglaf told Bragwort. "She is coming with us."

"To be our coach," Angus added.

Bragwort's mouth fell open. "A pig for a coach?" he cried. "I don't think so."

"Let us take a vote," Erica suggested.

"I am team captain," said Bragwort. "And I say no pig."

They stood outside the gatehouse, arguing.

At last Daisy said, "Old-hay it-yay, Agwort-bray. Et-lay ee-may ive-gay ou-yay a-yay ain-bray etcher-stray."

"What did she say?" asked Bragwort.

"Daisy wants to give you a brain stretcher," said Wiglaf.

"No, thanks," said Bragwort. "My brain is already stretched. It's huge!"

Daisy pretended not to hear. "Ou-yay and-yay ee-thray iends-fray are-shay a-yay ie-pay. At-whay action-fray of-yay e-thay ie-pay oes-day each-yay iend-fray et-gay?"

"Huh?" said Bragwort.

Wiglaf spoke up. "Daisy said, 'You and three friends share a pie. What fraction of the pie does each friend get?'"

"Easy," said Bragwort. "I get the whole pie, and my friends get nothing!" He laughed loudly.

"Ome-say enius-gay!" Daisy said, rolling her eyes.

"Is she saying how smart I am?" asked Bragwort.

Wiglaf nodded. "Daisy says you are a genius."

Bragwort beamed. "That is true," he said. "Oh, all right. I guess your pig can come with us if she really wants to."

Daisy winked at Wiglaf. Then she and the others followed Bragwort through the gatehouse and across the drawbridge. They were on their way to KNC!

Chapter 3

No moon shone that night. No stars, either. The trip through the Dark Forest was very dark indeed.

Strange birds cawed. Beasts growled in the brush. Hermits coughed and wheezed inside their caves. But Daisy gave the DSA team brain stretchers as they walked. This kept their minds from dwelling on the scary noises.

At last the sky grew light in the east.

"Zounds, Daisy!" Wiglaf exclaimed. "We are just north of Wizard's Bog. This is where we first met Zelnoc. Remember?"

"Es-yay," Daisy said stiffly. She had not forgiven the wizard for messing up her speech spell.

The party stopped for breakfast.

"Stone cold eel fries—ugh!" said Angus.

After breakfast, the DSA team walked on and on and on. By noon, Wiglaf had blisters. By suppertime, he had blisters on his blisters.

At sunset, they reached the top of a hill.

"There it is!" cried Erica, looking down. "Knights Noble Conservatory!"

"Ounds-zay!" exclaimed Daisy.

Angus whistled. "That is some fancy castle," he said.

"I wonder if I could transfer," Bragwort mused. "Someone as smart as I deserves to go to the finest school."

Wiglaf stared at KNC in silence. He had seen King Arthur's castle in Camelot. But this was even fancier. Its white stone glowed pink in the sunset. Wiglaf counted fourteen towers. Each flew a red-and-white KNC flag.

Angus straightened his tunic. Erica rubbed the dust off her boots. Bragwort spit on the tail of his tunic and scrubbed at the dirt on his face. Wiglaf tried to push his unruly carrot-colored hair under his cap. Only Daisy felt perfectly confident to enter KNC just the way she was.

The DSA team members made their way

down the hill to the KNC drawbridge. Two knights stood guard at the bridge. One wore shiny white armor. The other wore armor of red.

"Ello-hay!" Daisy greeted the knights.

"Egad!" said the red knight. "The pig speaks!"

"Is the swine under an enchantment?" asked the white knight.

Wiglaf nodded. "Her name is Daisy, and she is our coach."

"We are the Dragon Slayers' Academy team," Erica told the knights. "We are here to compete in the Brain-Power Tournament."

"You may cross the bridge." said the white knight. "See Jeeves inside the castle. He'll show you to your rooms."

The DSA team and their coach crossed the bridge. They walked through the KNC gatehouse and across the castle yard. Wiglaf had never seen such a green lawn. On the far side of the yard he spied several boys in red-and-white uniforms. They had mallets and were hitting a ball through little wickets.

"I hope we have come in time for supper," Angus muttered.

The DSA team walked into the castle. Wiglaf was amazed. The stone floors shone. Portraits of famous graduates hung on the walls. The first was a portrait of Sir Lancelot.

A tall, thin man with snow white hair hurried toward them. He had on a white velvet tunic and white gloves.

"Greetings," he said. "You must be..." He looked them up and down, and said, "...lost."

"We are not lost, sir," said Erica. She explained that they were the DSA team. And that Daisy was their coach.

"Oh, dear," the man muttered. Then he said, "I am Jeeves, head butler."

Butler? thought Wiglaf. He had never realized just how different DSA was from KNC.

They followed Jeeves down the hall to his office.

"Ah! I have just the room for you," Jeeves said as he checked a large book. "It has a lovely garden view."

"Oh, thank you, sir," said Wiglaf. He thought he could get used to this grand style of living.

Jeeves rang a bell on his desk.

Instantly, a servant decked out in the school colors appeared. He bowed to Jeeves.

"Take their luggage to Suite D, Otto," Jeeves said.

Otto frowned. "Surely, sir, you don't mean..."

"Oh, but I do," said Jeeves. "Suite D for DSA." He turned to the team. "A meeting to go over the rules will be held in the Sword-in-the-Stone Gymnasium at eight bells tonight. You just have time to go to your room and freshen up."

"What about supper, sir?" Angus asked eagerly.

"You have missed supper," Jeeves replied.

"But we are very hungry, sir," said Angus.

"The kitchen is closed," Jeeves said. "And we here at KNC do not believe in eating between meals."

Wiglaf thought he had never seen Angus look so disappointed. He still had his eel custard left in his own pack. He would share it with his friend.

Bragwort handed Otto his pack. Otto grabbed a torch from the wall and led the DSA team down the hallway. They came to a set of stairs leading up to one of the towers. But Otto turned and began leading them down a set of stairs. The hallway at the bottom looked nothing like the hallway upstairs. It was dark, for one thing. And it smelled funny.

"Here we are," said Otto. "Suite D." He turned a rusty key in the lock. The door squeaked open.

Wiglaf squinted into the room. Otto's torch lit it well enough for him to see four small cots shoved up against the wall.

"But-but-but..." Erica sputtered. "This is a dungeon!"

"We never call it that anymore," Otto told them. "And look." He pointed to the small, barred window way at the top of the wall. "In the daylight, you can see a bit of the garden."

Otto lit the lone torch on the wall, which made the little room very smoky. Then he bowed and vanished down the hallway.

"They can't do this to me!" Bragwort cried. "I am the team captain! I, at least, should have a better room!"

"Oh, pipe down, Bragwort," said Erica.

"I shall go talk to Jeeves," Bragwort said, storming off.

Erica began to pace up and down Suite D.

Angus sighed and sat down on a cot.

"Ow!" he cried. "This bed is hard as a rock!" He pulled up the thin blanket that covered it. "No wonder," he said. "It *is* a rock!"

Wiglaf sat down on the hard stone cot next to Angus's. He patted Daisy absently on the head.

Moments later, Bragwort stormed back into Suite D. Wiglaf guessed that his talk with Jeeves had not gone well.

"I say we go back to DSA!" Bragwort wailed.

"Quit?" Erica cried. "Never!" She kept pacing up and down. "We are going to show everyone what the DSA team is made of! We are going to stay and represent DSA in the All-Schools Brain-Power Tournament. And we are going to win!"

Chapter 4

ONG! BONG! BONG! BONG! BONG! BONG! BONG! BONG!

"That's eight," Angus said. "Let us be off. Perchance there will be snacks at this meeting."

The DSA team hurried out of the dungeon. They ran up the stairs. Wiglaf saw a huge boulder. The handle of a sword stuck out of it. He figured they had found the right spot.

The DSA team walked into the torch-lit gym.

"No snacks!" Angus moaned.

"Here comes the DSA team," called the red knight. "Take a seat on your bench, men!"

Four benches had been placed in a square in the middle of the gym. Three were already filled. Four boys sat on each bench with their coach. The DSA team quickly sat down on the only empty bench. Daisy plopped down on the floor beside Wiglaf.

The KNC team sat across from DSA. The KNC boys wore red silk tunics. Huge gold KNC medallions hung from gold chains around their necks. They wore red-and-white striped puffy pants, white leggings, and floppy white hats with large red plumes.

"The Knights Noble Conservatory team looks very fancy," Wiglaf whispered to Erica.

Erica shrugged. "Fancy doesn't mean smart."

Wiglaf glanced at the team to his left. They wore green felt hats bearing the letters DSP for Dragon Stabbers' Prep. Their green tunics had pockets. And in the pockets each team member carried several writing quills. All four DSP boys were thin and pale. They had ink-stained fingers. They did not look the sort to stab dragons. Rather, they looked as if they spent their time indoors. In a library, perhaps. Wiglaf thought they looked as if they would do very well in a brain-power tournament.

"Do you think the DSP team looks smart?" Wiglaf asked Erica.

Erica studied the boys for a moment.

"You can't always tell by looks," she said.

The Knights R Us team—four big, strapping lads—sat on the bench to Wiglaf's right. They wore yellow short-sleeved tunics. The letters KRU had been stitched onto their sleeves.

"Attention, lads!" the white knight said. "I now present the headmaster of Knights Noble Conservatory, Sir Verm!"

The boys clapped politely.

Sir Verm, tall and thin, stepped into the middle of the square made by the benches. His white silk cape was lined with red fur that matched his red hair.

"Welcome to Knights Noble Conservatory," the headmaster said. "Welcome to the Brain-Power Tournament. I'd like each team captain to stand now and introduce his team." He turned to his KNC boys. "Chauncy? Why don't you begin?"

Chauncy stood. "I am Chauncy," he said. "My team members are Launcy, Flauncy, and Delauncy. And this is our coach, Sir Worthing-ton-Smyth."

The boys and the coach stood as their names were called.

"I'd like to add," said Chauncy, "that KNC has won the Brain-Power Tournament for the last ninety-nine years. And tomorrow we are going to make it a hundred!"

The KNC boys clapped. Chauncy sat down.

Next, a boy in a green DSP tunic stood up. "I'm known as 200," he said. "These are my teammates, 170, 180, and 195. And this is our coach, Professor Plum."

Each DSP boy stood as his number was called.

"Most unusual," said Sir Verm. "Why do you go by numbers, 200?"

"The numbers are our IQs," explained 200. "Mine is highest. So I am captain. But anything over 150 is considered genius level."

200 sat down.

Wiglaf leaned toward Erica. "I knew they were smart," he whispered.

Erica shrugged again. "Numbers never tell the whole story," she said as a KRU boy stood up.

"I'm Lance," he said.

"Ah! Any relation to our most famous alum, Sir Lancelot?" asked Sir Verm eagerly.

"No, but one of these days I shall challenge Sir Lancelot to a duel," said Lance. "And when I win, I shall be the most famous Lance."

Erica rolled her eyes. "What an oversized ego!"

"My teammates," Lance went on, "are Spike, Duke, and Moose."

The KRU boys stood and flexed their muscles.

"And this is Coach Bruiser," Lance added.

The KRU coach flexed his muscles, too.

Now the headmaster turned to the DSA team. His eyes came to a stop at Daisy.

"This is no ordinary pig," Wiglaf said quickly. "Her name is Daisy. She speaks. And she is very well-read, which is why we made her our coach."

"Ello-hay, Ir-say Erm-vay," said Daisy.

"Good King Ken's britches!" the headmaster exclaimed.

"Sir?" said Chauncy. "No team has ever had a pig for a coach before. I think DSA should be disqualified."

"What?" Erica leapt to her feet. "Show me where it says *no pig coaches* in the rule book!"

"Having a pig coach is unusual," said the headmaster. "But it is not against the rules. Now, where is your captain?"

Bragwort stood and gave his name. "I could win this contest on my own," he said. "But the rules say there must be four team members. So I must put up with Eric, Angus, and Wiglaf."

The three stood as their names were called. Wiglaf saw that the KNC boys had their hands over their mouths to keep from giggling. The KRU boys were not even trying to hide their laughter. Wiglaf felt his face grow hot. Maybe they were a ragtag bunch. But Wiglaf vowed to show the other schools that DSA was a force to be reckoned with!

"Now we know who's who," said the headmaster as the DSA team sat down. "The tournament begins tomorrow morning at nine o'clock. Now, off you go, men. And tomorrow, may the best team win!"

"Wait a minute, sir!" Erica called out. "We have not yet gone over the tournament rules."

"Oh, you'll catch on, DSA," said Sir Verm. "Not that it really matters," he went on. "Odds are that KNC will win."

The KNC boys nodded. Wiglaf thought they did not even seem very excited about winning. They acted as if they knew they were going to win. And the tournament had not yet started!

"Now, if there are no more questions, you're dismissed," said Sir Verm. "Get a good night's sleep, men!"

Daisy, Erica, Angus, Wiglaf, and Bragwort made their way slowly back to Suite D. No one said anything on the way. Things did not look promising for the DSA team.

Erica lit the torch inside their chamber.

They all sat down on their cots. Silently, they took out what was left of their eel meal. Wiglaf shared his with Angus and Daisy. His pig was the only one who seemed happy with her fare.

"I know how we can win," Bragwort said, breaking the silence.

"How?" asked Wiglaf.

"*I* shall answer all the questions," Bragwort replied.

"Oh, go soak your head, Bragwort," Erica said. "We are a *team*. We shall work together."

"Do you not want to win?" Bragwort cried.

"Not like that," Erica replied. "Besides, we all know different things. For example, if there are questions on knighthood or jousting or armor, then *I* shall be the one to answer. And Angus shall answer if the category is food. And—"

"Do not talk of food!" Angus pleaded.

Wiglaf very much wanted to hear what category Erica thought he might answer. He had not done well on the S.A.T.-M.E. He was worried about doing his part for his team in the tournament. But Bragwort kept interrupting, so Erica never had a chance to say.

At last Erica snuffed out the torch. They all lay down on their cold stone cots.

"Get a good night's sleep. Ha!" Angus grumbled.

Daisy gave the DSA team more brain stretchers. Soon the sound of her soft Pig Latin lulled them all to sleep.

Chapter 5

"Breakfast!" Angus cried as he rolled out of bed the next morning. "I need breakfast!"

Wiglaf dressed quickly. Then he and the others followed Angus out of Suite D. Angus followed his nose to the KNC dining hall. But when he saw the chalkboard with the breakfast menu outside the door, he stopped short.

TODAY'S TOURNAMENT BREAKFAST
Scrambled eel eggs on toast
Fried eel bacon
Fresh squeezed eel juice

"Noooo," Angus moaned.

"Rotten luck," said Erica.

Just then a man in a white chef's hat hurried over to them.

"You must be from DSA," he said.

"We are," Angus said. "Pray, kind sir, have you nothing for breakfast beside eel, eel, eel?"

"Nothing." The cook smiled. "I am Frypot's cousin, Halfbake. Frypot sent me the message yesterday. He said eel would make you feel right at home here at KNC."

Angus let out a groan.

"Thank you," Wiglaf managed.

The DSA team skipped breakfast. Hungry and cranky, they made their way to the gym.

"This is your fault, Wiglaf," Angus said. "Never insult Frypot's lumpen pudding."

"Sorry," Wiglaf muttered.

Wiglaf, Angus, Erica, and even Daisy gasped as they walked into the gym. The place was full of people! KNC fans filled the benches in the biggest section. They wore white caps with red plumes and waved red-and-white flags.

The next section was filled with Dragon Stabbers' Prep fans. They held large green cards. Wiglaf saw that letters on them spelled out, GO, BRAINIACS!

Six cheerleaders stood near the KRU fans.

"Gimme a K!" the cheerleaders yelled.

"K!" shouted the KRU fans.

"Gimme an R!"

"R!"

"Gimme a U!"

"U!

"What's it spell?"

The KRU fans were silent. They scratched their heads, thinking hard.

"You can do it!" yelled the head cheerleader.

At last a fan called out, "K-R-U!"

"Yes!" screamed the cheerleaders. "What's it stand for?"

"Knights-R-Us!"

"Not a very clever cheer," Erica commented.

Wiglaf glanced at the fourth section of seats. A sign on the wall said DSA. But every bench in the DSA section was empty. Mordred had not sent a single fan to cheer them on.

"We must hold our heads up high as we walk to our places," Erica whispered to the team.

"Hey!" said Bragwort. "I'm the captain. I'm supposed to say things like that."

"Go ahead," said Erica.

"Um...heads up," Bragwort told the team.

Wiglaf tried to look proud as he marched. He felt the eyes of everyone in the room on them. He followed his teammates up a set of stairs onto the stage. They sat down on the bench labeled DSA. Daisy sat on the floor next to Wiglaf. A bell hung from a rope in front of the teams. Wiglaf thought it looked a bit closer to the KNC team than to any of the others.

Wiglaf looked over his shoulder. The red knight and the white knight stood at the back of the stage holding a large wheel. Beside them, a scoreboard listed the four teams. Otto sat on the side of the stage holding a horn, a drum, and a gong.

Wiglaf glanced at the DSA seats again.

"Zounds!" he exclaimed, pointing to a lone fan. "Brother Dave has come!"

The DSA team waved to the monk.

Brother Dave smiled and waved back.

"Thou can win!" he called.

Now Sir Verm strode to center stage.

"Welcome to the One-Hundredth All-Schools Brain-Power Tournament," he said. "Today, these young scholars shall match wits with one another. I think I can promise you an exciting contest. I know one team is in peak condition." He smiled at the KNC boys. They beamed back at him.

"Playing favorites already," Angus muttered.

"O-nay idding-kay," muttered Daisy.

"The categories in our tournament are chosen at random from lists of questions submitted by faculty members from each school," said Sir Verm. "And now, let me introduce the gentleman who has been hosting our tournament for a quarter century, Harkbert!"

The fans clapped and screamed as the famous host Harkbert walked onto the stage. He wore a shiny black cape.

"Greetings students and teachers!" said Harkbert. "Greetings coaches and teams! And now, let the tournament begin! KNC?" He nodded toward the home team. "I believe you always start things off."

Chauncy stood up.

Otto began beating on his drum.

"Knights!" called Harkbert. "The wheel, please!"

Chapter 6

he red knight and the white knight stepped forward holding the big wheel. Wiglaf saw six categories written on it. But before he had a chance to read them, Chauncy gave the wheel a spin. Then he sat down.

Around and around the wheel went. At last it stopped. An arrow at the top of the wheel pointed to NAME THAT HERO.

"The first question in each category is worth ten points," Harkbert explained. "The second question, twenty points. The third question, thirty points. And so on up to the fifth question. The first scholar to ring the bell gets a chance to answer the first question. If he answers correctly, his team continues answering questions until they miss one. Then the question is thrown open to the other teams."

Harkbert cleared his throat.

"This hero slew twelve mean, nasty-smelling dragons in the year 289," he said. "He was known as Sir Dirty Dozen. For ten points, name that hero!"

Wiglaf had no idea who this ancient hero might be. Clearly the questions at this tournament were going to be very hard.

But Delauncy sprang up right away. He rang the bell.

"Sir Dirk of Dirkingsmop," he called.

"Correct," Harkbert said.

"Atta boy, Delauncy!" called Sir Verm.

Wiglaf was impressed.

A page ran over to the scoreboard. He hung a 10 under KNC. The KNC fans called:

> *Rah, rah, rah for good old red and white!*
> *Rah, rah, rah for we are always right!*

"A hero is buried in Sir Mandrake's tomb," said Harkbert. "For twenty points, name that hero!"

What an easy question! thought Wiglaf.

Launcy rang the bell and yelled, "Sir Mandrake!"

"Correct!" cried Harkbert.

The KNC score rose to 30.

"This hero's name begins with the letter L. Part of his name is also the name of a weapon," said Harkbert. "For thirty points, name that hero!"

Wiglaf looked at Erica and rolled his eyes. Anybody could answer this one.

Delauncy was first to reach the bell.

"Sir Lancelot!" he cried.

"Correct!" said Harkbert.

Suddenly Otto banged his gong.

BONG!!

"That's the bonus gong!" Harkbert exclaimed. "KNC answered the last question correctly so the question goes to them. For 500 bonus points, where did this hero go to school?"

Flauncy hopped up and rang the bell. He shouted, "KNC!"

"Right again!" exclaimed Harkbert.

The page changed the KNC score to 560.

"Now back to the wheel," said Harkbert.

The KNC boys answered every NAME THAT

HERO question correctly. By the end of the first round, their score was 650. No other team had any score at all.

"No wonder they win every year," Erica grumbled. "No one else gets a turn."

It was time for a new category. Chauncy spun the wheel again. It landed on TABLE MANNERS.

"For ten points," said Harkbert, "name two eating utensils."

Delauncy raced to the bell. "Spoon and knife!" he said.

"That's right!" said Harkbert.

Wiglaf shook his head. Nobody else even had a chance to answer. Suddenly Wiglaf began to understand. Nobody else was supposed to get a turn. That first question had been hard on purpose. Wiglaf bet that KNC had been given the answer. No wonder they were winning!

Chauncy, Launcy, Flauncy, and Delauncy whipped through TABLE MANNERS. They did the same with FANCY DANCE STEPS. And FINE POINTS OF CROQUET. After the lunch break—eel fritters on a bun—KNC gave the right answers to every question in the AMUSING LATIN VERSES category.

Otto banged the bonus gong again, and KNC earned 500 bonus points. Their score kept going up and up and up.

The other teams' scores stayed at nothing.

Late in the afternoon, Wiglaf glanced at Brother Dave. The monk waved. "Go thou DSA!" he called.

But Wiglaf thought he looked worried.

Now the category was FASHION. KNC had answered two questions correctly.

Harkbert said, "For thirty points, name a silver decoration used to fasten a shoe."

Flauncy rang the bell. "A strap!" he yelled.

Sir Verm stood up. "Want to try again, Flaunce?" he asked.

Daisy groaned. "O-nay air-fay!"

"I am sorry," said Harkbert. "No second chances."

Otto blew a small horn: TOOT.

Flauncy folded his arms over his chest. "Fooey!" he said.

"The question is now open to the other teams," said Harkbert.

Yes! thought Wiglaf. *At last!*

Erica lunged for the bell.

But Bragwort beat her to it: DING!

"Yes, Bragwort?" said Harkbert.

"A hook!" Bragwort yelled.

Harkbert shook his head. "Wrong."

Wiglaf groaned silently. This was DSA's chance to get in the game—and Bragwort had blown it!

Now Spike on the KRU team rang the bell. "A buckle!" he shouted.

"Yes!" said Harkbert. "Thirty points for KRU!"

With that the KRU cheerleaders jumped to their feet. They shouted:

> *Nonnie nonnie poo poo*
> *We are gonna beat you!*

"The next question is yours, KRU," said Harkbert. "For forty points, what do you call a fashionable ladies' hairstyle in which three clumps of hair are woven together?"

Moose rang the bell and yelled, "A ponytail!"

"I'm sorry," said Harkbert. "Wrong answer. The question is open to the other teams."

Now Wiglaf lunged for the bell.

But Bragwort beat him to it.

"A pageboy!" Bragwort yelled.

Wiglaf's mouth fell open. He could not believe it! Bragwort had done it again!

"Sorry, DSA," said Harkbert.

The boy named 170 from DSP rang the bell.

"Braids!" he yelled.

"That's it, 170!" said Harkbert. "Forty points for DSP."

The DSP fans yelled:

> *When it comes to brains,*
> *We've really got a lot!*
> *That's why we shall win,*
> *And that's why you shall not!*

Then DSP went on to answer the fifth FASHION question correctly.

Wiglaf glanced at the scoreboard. It said:

KNC	DSP	KRU	DSA
1780	90	30	0

Harkbert said, "That was the last question on *this side* of the wheel. But before we end the first day of the tournament, I shall ask one last question—from the *back side* of the wheel."

A murmur went up from the crowd. Wiglaf could tell that they expected something exciting to happen.

"Knights!" said Harkbert. "Turn the wheel!"

Otto beat his drum. The knights turned the back side of the wheel face out.

Wiglaf's eyes lit up as he read the new categories:

WIN A TRIP TO CAMELOT
WIN A DATE WITH A PRINCESS
WIN 1,000 POINTS

But he gasped as he read on:

WIN A TRIP TO PLAGUE-RAT VILLAGE
WIN A DATE WITH A DRAGON
LOSE 1,000 POINTS

Wiglaf swallowed. Clearly the back of the wheel was risky. But DSA had to take a chance. It was their only hope of winning.

"The drumroll, Otto," said Harkbert.

Otto began beating his drum again.

"Spin the wheel!" said Harkbert.

The red knight twirled the wheel.

"Is anyone bold enough to play the bonus round?" Harkbert challenged the scholars. "Is anyone brave enough to ring the bell?"

Wiglaf nudged Erica.

"You must ring the bell," he whispered.

"This is a wheel of misfortune!" Erica whispered back.

"Yes," Wiglaf agreed. "But it is our only chance! You are the smartest one on our team. You must play!"

"You're right," Erica said. She sprang to her feet and started for the bell, but...

DING!

Wiglaf couldn't believe it!

Bragwort had rung the bell!

Harkbert smiled. "Hurry on up here, lad, while the wheel is still spinning."

Bragwort bounced eagerly up to the wheel.

Wiglaf watched in horror as the wheel began to slow down. It passed WIN A DATE WITH A PRINCESS. It passed WIN 1,000 POINTS. It kept going slowly, slowly. It passed WIN A TRIP TO PLAGUE-RAT VILLAGE. It squeaked by WIN A DATE

WITH A DRAGON and came to a stop on LOSE 1,000 POINTS.

"If you answer your question correctly," said Harkbert, "your score stays as it is. But if your answer is wrong, your team will lose a thousand points. Are you ready?"

"Ready!" cried Bragwort.

"Finish this rhyme," said Harkbert. "Thirty days hath September, April, June and—"

Wiglaf gave a sigh of relief. Easy question!

Harkbert looked at Bragwort expectantly.

Otto began beating his drum.

"Ou-yay an-cay o-day it-yay, Agwort-bray!" breathed Daisy.

"Uh...could you repeat the question?" asked Bragwort.

"Certainly," said Harkbert. "Thirty days hath September, April, June and—"

Bragwort scratched his head. He pressed his lips together. He squeezed his eyes shut. Clearly, he was thinking hard.

TOOT! Otto blew his horn.

"I'm sorry. Time's up!" said Harkbert.

"Febtober!" Bragwort yelled.

Febtober? Wiglaf smacked himself on the head. Surely Bragwort must have a minus 1,000 IQ!

Harkbert shook his head. "The answer is 'November.' But nice try from the DSA team."

"Thank you, sir," said Bragwort. He shrugged to his teammates. "We had no points to lose anyway," he whispered as he took his place on the bench again.

"Oh, no?" growled Erica. "Take a look at the scoreboard!"

Everyone was looking as the page fixed the final scores for the first day of the tournament:

KNC	DSP	KRU	DSA
1780	90	30	U.O. 1000

Bragwort frowned. "Sir Verm!" he called. "What does the score U.O. 1,000 mean?"

"It means, DSA," said Sir Verm, "that *you owe* one thousand pieces of gold."

"And that," said Harkbert, "ends the first day of our tournament. We'll see everyone back here tomorrow morning!"

Chapter 7

ooh, I'm so glad I'm not you, Bragwort," Angus said as the DSA team left the gym.

"So I missed one," said Bragwort. "Big deal."

"But, Bragwort," Wiglaf said. "Mordred is coming tomorrow. He expects us to have *won* gold for him."

"He won't be happy when he finds out that he *owes* gold to KNC," Erica added.

"It was a hard question," Bragwort whined.

Just then Brother Dave hurried over to them.

"Eetings-gray, Aisy-day," he said. He gave the pig a pat. Then he turned to the DSA team. "Be ye not sorrowful, lads. 'Tis only a game, after all." He shook his head. "Thou knowest I try not to find fault with others, for none of us is perfect. But..." He lowered his voice. "...the categories today did seem to favor a certain team. Fine points of croquet, indeed!"

"And table manners!" Erica rolled her eyes.

Brother Dave nodded. "But thou must not lose heart, lads," he said. "For thou canst never tell what tomorrow may bring."

Brother Dave murmured something about going to chapel. He hurried away.

"And *I* am going to the KNC school store," Bragwort said. "I shall buy myself a fine red-and-white KNC souvenir tunic."

Then he rushed off.

"Good. Bragwort is gone," Erica said to Wiglaf and Angus. "We must figure out how to stop him from ringing the bell tomorrow!"

They ran down to Suite D. Wiglaf lit the torch. He coughed as the room grew smoky.

"I can think of only one way to stop Bragwort," said Erica.

"What?" asked Wiglaf.

"Tie him up, stuff a sock in his mouth, and lock him in here," she said.

"But we must have a full team to play," Angus pointed out.

Erica frowned. "But if he is onstage, how can we stop him from ringing the bell?"

"A spell," Wiglaf said. "We could summon Zelnoc."

"Summon quickly, Wiggie," said Erica. "We haven't much time."

Wiglaf closed his eyes. He chanted the wizard's name backwards three times: "Conlez! Conlez! Conlez!"

When he opened his eyes, he saw smoke. Torch smoke. Red smoke. Blue smoke. Yellow, green, and violet smoke.

"Holy smoke!" cried a voice that Wiglaf recognized as the wizard's. "Somebody open a window!"

"We can't!" came Angus's voice. "This is a dungeon!"

"Oh, jester's bells," cried Zelnoc. "Just let me get my wand out of my sleeve...."

Wiglaf blinked. The smoke was vanishing into the tip of the wizard's wand.

"That's better," Zelnoc said at last. He looked around. "Say, do you folks want me to do a little wallpaper spell? Something with a floral pattern would cheer the place up. How long are you in for, anyway?"

"We are just visiting," Wiglaf told him.

"Good gizzards!" the wizard exclaimed. "You again, Wiglof!"

"Hello, sir," said Wiglaf.

"Stop!" Zelnoc put his hands over his ears. "I know you want something. You always do. But don't tell me what it is. You managed to summon me from Zizmor's new mind-reading seminar. The least you can do is give me a chance to see how I'm doing."

Zelnoc closed his eyes. He put his fingers to his forehead. He stayed that way for a while. "I'm getting a blank here, Woglip," he said at last. "You must *think* about what you want. Or I have nothing to read inside your mind."

Wiglaf thought of Bragwort ringing the bell. Bragwort yelling out answers. Bragwort losing 1,000 points for DSA.

"I'm getting it now," said Zelnoc. "You have a wart. But...why are you bragging about it?"

"I was thinking of Bragwort, sir," said Wiglaf. "He is our team captain."

"What team?" asked Zelnoc.

"The DSA team," Wiglaf told him. "We are competing in the All-Schools Brain-Power Tournament."

"Go on," Zelnoc said.

"Bragwort keeps ringing the bell so he can answer questions," Erica put in. "But he doesn't know the answers."

Zelnoc brightened. "I could put my famous no-bell ringing spell on him," the wizard said. "I won an award for inventing that spell. Yes, sir, my fellow enchanters gave me the No-Bell Prize." Zelnoc smiled at the memory. Then he shook his head. "But this Bragwort might still call out answers."

"He *would* call out," Angus said. "That is so like him."

Erica nodded. "He is such a know-it-all."

"A know-it-all!" said Zelnoc. "Why didn't you say so? I've got just the thing! Now where do I find this boy?"

"What boy?" came a voice from the door of Suite D. There stood Bragwort holding a bag from the KNC School Store.

"Do you answer to the name of Bragwort?" asked Zelnoc.

"So, you have heard of me." Bragwort smiled. "Is it because of my sky-high score on the S.A.T.–M.E.? Or because of my boldness here at the brain-power tournament?"

"Never mind how," said Zelnoc. He aimed his wand at Bragwort, and began to sing:

"Do, re, me, fa, sol, la, ti!
Wise as an owl you wish to be.
Ti, la, sol, fa, me, re, do!
Wise as an owl, it shall be so."

A small puff of smoke spurted from the tip of Zelnoc's wand.

Bragwort simply stared at the wizard. For once he seemed to have nothing to say.

"That's it?" Erica asked the wizard.

"Short and simple," said Zelnoc. "But very effective." He turned to Wiglaf. "I've got to get back to Zizmor's seminar now. I was right in the middle of reading a very interesting mind. Hope I can find my place. Ta-ta, Woglip."

"Wait, wizard!" Erica cried. "If Bragwort

knows all, then we shall win, but not by fair play!"

Wiglaf sighed. Sometimes Erica took rules far too seriously.

But Zelnoc had begun to spin. He spun faster and faster. Then—*poof*! He vanished in a burst of yellow smoke.

"Rats!" Erica exclaimed. "He never even answered me."

"Who?" said Bragwort.

"The wizard," said Erica.

"Zelnoc always makes a fast getaway," Angus observed.

"Who?" said Bragwort.

"Zelnoc!" said Erica, sounding annoyed.

Wiglaf stared at Bragwort. He did not look any different since Zelnoc had put the spell on him. But Wiglaf was beginning to think that maybe he had changed in some small way.

"Bragwort?" said Wiglaf. "How do you feel?"

"Who?" said Bragwort.

"You," said Wiglaf.

"Who?" said Bragwort.

"Uh-oh," said Wiglaf.

Chapter 8

Wiglaf, Angus, and Erica stared at Bragwort.

Bragwort did not seem to notice. He busied himself putting on his new red-and-white souvenir tunic.

"You look very nice in it, Bragwort," Angus told him.

"Who?" said Bragwort.

"You," said Angus.

"Bragwort," said Erica, "can you say anything besides 'who?'"

"Who?" said Bragwort.

"Oh, jester's bells!" Erica exclaimed. "Bragwort isn't as *wise* as an owl. He only *sounds* like an owl!" She turned to Wiglaf. "Summon that no-good wizard again," she growled. "And fast!"

"Conlez! Conlez! Conlez!" said Wiglaf.

Nothing happened.

"Conlez! Conlez! Conlez!" cried Angus.

No wizard appeared.

"Rats!" said Erica. "He must have turned off his summoner. Wizards aren't supposed to do that."

"Who?" said Bragwort.

"The wiz—Oh, will you stop it, Bragwort?" Erica cried.

"Who?" said Bragwort.

"YOU!" cried Erica. "Stop talking!"

"Woe is us!" Angus wailed. "How can we be in the tournament tomorrow with Bragwort saying nothing but who, who, who?"

Wiglaf flopped down on his cot.

"Ow!" he cried. He had forgotten that the bed was stone. Sometimes he wished he had never met Zelnoc.

There was nothing to do but get some sleep. But even that was hard with Bragwort *who who whooing* all night long.

The next morning the DSA team nibbled a few crusts of eel toast for breakfast. Then they found Brother Dave outside the Sword-in-the-Stone Gym.

"Brother Dave!" cried Angus. "We are in big trouble."

And he told the DSA librarian their latest tale of woe.

Brother Dave looked at Bragwort through his small, round glasses. "What does thou sayeth, Bragwort?" he asked.

"Who?" said Bragwort.

"Thou," said Brother Dave.

"Who?" said Bragwort.

"Oh, my," said Brother Dave. "Thou dost have a problem."

"If only Bragwort hadn't hogged the bell," Erica said. "Then we wouldn't be in this mess."

"If only Bragwort hadn't answered the question on the back of the wheel," said Angus.

Wiglaf sighed. "If only Zelnoc hadn't messed up his spell."

"Oh, my fine lads," said Brother Dave, shaking his head. "Folks say, 'If wishes were horses then beggars would ride.' 'If,' indeed! Wishes are not horses. Thou must not pin thy hopes on if, if, if. But thou are smart lads. And good thinking shall serve thee well in the end. Count on what thou knowest! Never give up hope. And remember: 'if' meaneth nothing!"

Wiglaf tried to be hopeful as he followed his teammates into the gym. There was not an empty seat in the place—except for the whole DSA section. The DSA team owed 1,000 points. The DSA team captain could say only, "Who?"

At least, thought Wiglaf as he took his seat upon the stage, *things could hardly get worse.*

"Welcome to day two of the Brain-Power Tournament," said Sir Verm. "As you can see from the scoreboard, Knights Noble Conservatory is ahead. And, as usual, the other teams are behind." Sir Verm turned the stage over to Harkbert.

"All right, knights," Harkbert said. "Bring in the wheel with today's question categories."

The knights stepped forward with the wheel.

A murmur rose from the crowd.

Sir Verm's eyes bugged out as he stared at the wheel.

Wiglaf's eyes widened, too. For the categories were a bit more down-to-earth today. They were: SIR LANCELOT, DRAGON STATS, JOUSTING, FINE DINING, WASHING DISHES, and CABBAGE FARMING. Wiglaf smiled. He was an expert in two out of six of the categories. If only he could get a turn.... He stopped himself. He thought about Brother Dave's little talk. He must not count on 'if.' He must simply lunge for the bell!

"Zounds!" Sir Verm exclaimed. "What categories are these?" He frowned at the knights. "I had fixed it so that... I mean, I had fixed my hopes on *other* categories. The more usual categories, if you see what I mean."

"We picked these categories from the category box this morning, sir," the red knight told the headmaster. "The monk there—" he nodded toward Brother Dave "—happened to be backstage when we were picking the categories, if you see what I mean, sir."

Sir Verm frowned. He shot Brother Dave a dirty look. But he said nothing.

Brother Dave only smiled and raised his eyes heavenward.

Wiglaf thought it very lucky indeed that Brother Dave had been backstage at just the right moment.

The white knight handed Harkbert the answer sheets.

The KNC headmaster managed to sit down.

"Chauncy," said Harkbert, "spin the wheel."

Chauncy spun it.

It stopped on CABBAGE FARMING.

Wiglaf got ready to lunge in case KNC missed.

"For ten points," said Harkbert, "what do you call the tool used for breaking up soil clods before planting cabbage seeds?"

Chauncy wrinkled his nose. "What are soil clods?"

"Can you answer the question, Chauncy?" asked Harkbert.

"About cabbage farming?" Chauncy said. "I don't think so."

Otto blew his whistle: Toot!

"The question is open to other teams," said Harkbert.

Wiglaf dove for the bell.

But Bragwort beat him to it.

Ding!

"Who!" cried Bragwort.

Harkbert scowled. "Let me hear that answer again."

Erica leaped up and ran to Bragwort's side. Her hand quickly flew to Bragwort's mouth. She was trying to silence him. But as her hand clamped down over his mouth, Bragwort managed to shout out, "Wh-oh!"

"Correct," said Harkbert. "The answer is *hoe*."

Wiglaf watched the page hang a new score on the board for DSA: U.O. 990.

It was hardly a winning score. But it was a start. Wiglaf slapped hands with Erica as she sat down on the bench again.

Now Brother Dave stood up. He cupped his hands to his mouth and said loudly,

Go thou, DSA,
Fair school of fair play,
Thou shalt answer well today,
Go thou DSA!

Wiglaf grinned. Brother Dave was cheering them on!

"Next question to DSA," said Harkbert. "For twenty points, what do you call a single cabbage plant?"

Angus grabbed Bragwort's hands as Wiglaf dove for the bell. He hit it an instant before Bragwort wiggled out of Angus's grip.

DING!

"A head of cabbage!" Wiglaf cried.

"Correct," said Harkbert.

"Who, who, whooo," Bragwort whimpered.

Wiglaf hoped that Angus could hold on to Bragwort.

"For thirty points," said Harkbert, "what causes dark spots to appear on cabbage leaves?"

"Cabbage mold!" said Wiglaf.

"Correct!" said Harkbert.

Wiglaf grinned. He remembered reading the

passage in the S.A.T.-M.E. Maybe mold was his friend after all!

"For forty points," said Harkbert, "name the three main uses for cabbages."

"Cabbage soup, cabbage dumplings, and cole slaw!" cried Wiglaf.

"Yahoo!" cried Angus. "Go Wiggie!"

For the last, fifty-point question in the cabbage-farming category, Wiglaf named the spot where the world's biggest cabbage was grown: his own hometown, Pinwick. He earned 140 points in all for his team. The DSA score was now U.O. 850. Wiglaf got to spin the wheel for the next category. The arrow landed on FINE DINING.

"For ten points," said Harkbert, "name a food that begins with the letter C."

Angus hit the bell. "Chocolate!" he cried.

"Correct," said Harkbert. "Ten points for DSA."

"No fair!" whined Delauncy. "We're not getting our turn!"

All at once Otto banged his gong.

BONG!

"There's the bonus gong," said Harkbert. "DSA, for 500 points, name three desserts made with the ingredient just named!"

Angus grinned. "Chocolate pudding," he said.

"That's one," said Harkbert.

"Chocolate-chip cookies," said Angus.

"That's two," said Harkbert.

"And," said Angus, "devil's food cake!"

"That's three!" said Harkbert.

DSA owed only 340 points now. Hope sprang up in Wiglaf's heart. Maybe there was a chance for their team after all.

"Go, Angus!" Erica cried.

Angus did, indeed, go. He answered every question in the FINE DINING category. He brought the DSA score down to U.O. 200. When he spun the wheel again, it landed on SIR LANCELOT.

"That's more like it!" cried the whole KNC team.

Harkbert cleared his throat and said, "What is the most unusual feature of Sir Lancelot's armor?"

Erica quickly hit the bell.

But Chauncy sprang to his feet. "The extra flaps over his kneecaps," he yelled.

"Wrong," said Harkbert. "And you were out of turn, Chauncy."

Sir Verm stood. "It was a new category, Harkbert," the KNC headmaster said. "I think it's high time my boys were back in the game."

"Then they must get back in fair and square," said Harkbert. He nodded to Erica. "I shall repeat the question. What is the most unusual feature of Sir Lancelot's armor?"

"A tiny bud vase just above his heart," Erica said. "In it he puts the violet bouquets that damsels give to him."

"Correct," said Harkbert. "For twenty points, what is Sir Lancelot's full name?"

Again Erica hit the bell. "Lancelot du Lac," she said. "It means 'of the lake.'"

"Everybody knows that," grumbled Chauncy.

"For thirty points," said Harkbert, "what is the name of Sir Lancelot's twin brother?"

Erica rang the bell. "Leon!"

Erica answered every Sir Lancelot question.

Now the DSA score was U.O. 50. Erica spun the wheel. It landed on WASHING DISHES.

"For ten points," said Harkbert, "put these words in the correct order: rinse, dry, wash."

Now Wiglaf sprang forward and rang the bell. "Wash, rinse, dry!" he said.

"Correct," said Harkbert. "For twenty points, what do you call the soapy bubbles in a dish pan?"

"Suds!" cried Wiglaf.

"Huh?" said Chauncy. "What's suds?"

Launcy, Flauncy and Delauncy only shrugged.

Wiglaf grinned. Clearly the other schools did not have Scrubbing Class. He had never liked it much himself. But now it was coming in handy!

BONG! BONG! went Otto's gong.

"It's the double bonus!" cried Harkbert.

"DSA, for 1,000 points, what is the toughest kind of grease to clean off a skillet?"

Wiglaf hit the bell.

"Grease from wild boar sausages!" he said.

"Correct!" cried Harkbert.

"Go, DSA!" shouted Brother Dave. "Thou art back in the game!"

"Right you are, Brother," said Harkbert. "We have here a scholar who knows his dishwashing. We shall break for lunch now," he added. "Our score at this time is: KNC: 1,780 DSP: 90 KRU: 30 DSA: 980."

Everyone clapped. Brother Dave clapped so hard that his glasses fell off. The crowd began leaving the gym for lunch.

Wiglaf smiled. He hardly dared believe it. Brother Dave was right. DSA was back in the game.

Suddenly a large shadow fell over the DSA team.

On the stage before them stood Mordred. He scowled at the DSA team. His face was red with rage.

"What's this on the scoreboard?" growled the greedy headmaster. "DSA is in *second* place?"

"But, sir, we—" Erica began.

"Silence!" boomed Mordred. "I suggest you get ahead of KNC. And I mean right away! Or you'll spend the rest of your lives rotting away in my dungeon!"

Chapter 9

ordred glared at the DSA team.

"We...we must go to lunch now, Uncle Mordred," Angus said.

"Lunch?" Mordred boomed. "I forbid you even to *think* about lunch at a time like this!"

"We are hungry, Uncle," Angus said. "For we have not had—"

"Enough!" Mordred yelled.

"That's right," whimpered Angus.

"Forget about lunch! You stay here and practice for the next round," Mordred said.

"Who?" said Bragwort.

"All of you," Mordred replied. "Go on. Practice!"

"But there is no way to practice, sir," Erica said.

"For we do not know what the questions will be," Wiglaf added.

Mordred stroked his beard thoughtfully. "Would it help if I got copies of the questions for you?" he asked.

"But, sir!" said Erica. "That would be cheating. And no DSA student would ever stoop that low."

"Oh, cheating, schmeating," said Mordred. "What we want here is the gold. Stay put," he added. "I shall see what I can do."

So saying, the DSA headmaster hurried away.

"Ohhh," groaned Angus. "If I do not get something to eat soon, I shall perish."

"Do not perish yet," Erica advised. "For we are making a comeback in the tournament."

"Who?" said Bragwort.

"Us," said Erica before she caught herself.

"I'm going to the cafeteria," Angus said. He stood up.

"But Mordred said to stay here," Erica said.

"Mordred, schmordred," said Angus. "I need lunch."

"Too late for that," said Wiglaf. "Look. The fans are already coming back."

And so they were. The other teams took their places on the stage. Wiglaf glanced at the scoreboard. DSA was not too far behind KNC. If their luck held...If Bragwort could be kept quiet... *No,* he thought to himself. *No if's. If meant nothing.*

Sir Verm walked to center stage. "We come now to the last part of our tournament," he said. "We have a new set of categories on our wheel. And remember, our prize money doubles in this last round."

Once more the KNC Headmaster turned the stage over to Harkbert.

"It has come to my attention," Harkbert said, "that there has been some holding back of an eager bell ringer on the DSA team."

Wiglaf saw Chauncy's sly grin. It wasn't hard to guess who had tattled to Harkbert.

"I'll call a foul if I see any more of that," said Harkbert.

Wiglaf's heart sank. Bragwort was fast. If no one held him back, he would ring the bell. And their winning streak would quickly end.

"Knights!" cried Harkbert. "The wheel! DSA, your spin."

Wiglaf walked over to the wheel. He gave it a spin. He watched as the arrow came to rest on Fun With Words.

Wiglaf sat down again.

"For twenty points," said Harkbert, "name a pronoun."

Easy! thought Wiglaf. He reached for the bell. But he was not fast enough.

Bragwort got there first. Ding!

Oh no! Erica, Wiglaf, and Angus looked at each other in horror. But there was nothing they could do.

"Who!" he cried.

"Correct," said Harkbert. Wiglaf gasped with relief. "For forty points, name a word that rhymes with *shoe.*"

Bragwort hit the bell again.

"Who!" he cried.

"Right again," said Harkbert.

Wiglaf was stunned. Bragwort was actually winning points for them.

"For sixty points, what word sounds very like the call of a barn owl?"

"Who!" screeched Bragwort.

"Go for the gold, boy!" shouted Mordred.

"For eighty points," said Harkbert, "fill in the blank in this sentence. A *sentry* most often says: '_____ goes there?'"

"Who!" cried Bragwort.

"Yes," said Harkbert. "And now, for one hundred points, say the word that comes next when a jokester says, 'Knock, knock!'"

"WHO!" cried Bragwort.

"Correct," said Harkbert.

"That's the way, Bragwort!" Mordred cried.

Wiglaf glanced at the scoreboard as the page added Bragwort's 300 points. DSA now had 1,280. Bragwort had come through for the team!

BONG! BONG! BONG!

"There goes the gong for the Triple Bonus!" said Harkbert. "Every team will write down their answer to this bonus question."

Otto began passing out the parchment and quills to the team captains.

"Triple bonus questions are questions that have puzzled scholars for ages," said Harkbert.

"You shall have three minutes to discuss the matter with your teammates and write down an answer. If you answer correctly, you triple your score. If you choose not to answer, your score stays the same. But if your answer is wrong, you lose all your points." Harkbert turned to the fans. "Let's cheer our scholars on, folks!"

The fans went wild, cheering and clapping.

Wiglaf heard Mordred's voice boom out above the others, "Get it right, DSA—or else!"

But the last words Wiglaf heard before the crowd quieted came from Brother Dave.

"I have faith in thee, lads!" the monk cried.

Harkbert picked up a rolled parchment from a tray. Slowly, he opened it.

Otto began beating on his drum.

"Here is the Triple Bonus Question," Harkbert said. His voice was hardly more than a whisper. He met the gaze of each young scholar. Then he lowered his eyes and read aloud the Triple Bonus Question: "How much wood could a woodchuck chuck if a woodchuck could chuck wood?"

Chapter 10

Wiglaf scratched his head. He knew nothing about woodchucks. He knew even less about chucking wood. This was one tough question!

Harkbert picked up an hourglass. He turned it upside down. Grains of sand began sliding from the top of the glass to the bottom.

Otto began playing a bouncy tune on his horn.

> Deeter, deeter, deeter, deeter,
> Deeter, deeter, deet!
> Dee dee dee dee dee!
> Dada dada dada....

Wiglaf, Angus, and Erica put their heads together.

"Come on, Bragwort," Erica whispered.

"Who?" said Bragwort.

"You!" Erica grabbed his arm and pulled him over to them.

"Anybody know anything about woodchucks?" asked Erica.

No one said a word.

Not even Bragwort.

"I have a second cousin named Chuck," said Angus. "And I saw a woodchuck once," he added. "But he wasn't chucking wood."

"If a woodchuck could chuck wood," Wiglaf murmured, repeating the lines to himself. And suddenly he broke into a smile. "If a woodchuck could chuck wood!" he whispered. "'If!' It's just as Brother Dave said. *If* means nothing. *If* a woodchuck could chuck wood doesn't mean that a woodchuck *does* chuck wood."

"Wiggie's right," said Erica. "So the answer is..."

"None," Erica, Wiglaf, and Angus whispered at the same time.

"Okay, Bragwort," Erica said. "You're our team captain."

"Who?" said Bragwort.

"You!" said Erica. "So you have to write down the answer. None."

Bragwort picked up the quill and started writing.

Before long, Otto's tune ended:

Dit dit dit dit do do do!

"The sand has run out of the glass," said Harkbert. "Time's up! DSP? Do you have an answer?"

200 held up their parchment. It said, *Woodchucks, also known as "groundhogs," are members of the rodent family and are capable of chucking an absolutely enormous quantity of wood because of the way their teeth are...*

200 shrugged. "We ran out of time, sir," he said.

"I see." Harkbert nodded. "That is not correct. KRU?"

Lance held up the KRU parchment. It said, *A woodchuck chucks until a woodchuck upchucks!*

At this, the audience cracked up. It took some time for Harkbert to quiet everyone.

"That is not correct, KRU," said Harkbert. "KNC? Your answer, please."

Chauncy held up the KNC parchment. It said *12 Big Trees*.

"I'm sorry, KNC," said Harkbert. "That is not correct, either."

Everyone in the gym gasped. Was KNC going to lose all their points?

Wiglaf's heart began to pound with excitement. If DSA got it right, they would win a huge pot of gold for Mordred. And honor and glory for their team!

Wiglaf tried not to smile. Now was their turn to shine! He glanced over at the parchment in Bragwort's hand. He gasped!

Bragwort had written *Who who who* all over the parchment.

Wiglaf shook his head at Bragwort.

But Bragwort pressed his lips together. He looked very stubborn.

"DSA?" said Harkbert. "What is your answer?"

It was too late to change Bragwort's answer now.

Bragwort raised the parchment.

Quickly, Wiglaf grabbed the parchment and flipped it over.

Bragwort held up the parchment. But he was showing Harkbert its backside. And that side was blank.

"You seem to be holding up a parchment with nothing on it," said Harkbert.

"Who?" said Bragwort.

"You," said Harkbert.

"That is our answer, sir," Wiglaf said. "Nothing."

Harkbert raised his eyebrows. "So...that is your answer?"

"Yes, sir," said Wiglaf. "The parchment is blank because the answer is none."

"You better be right, boy!" Mordred yelled.

Harkbert smiled. "And you *are* right, DSA!" he said. "You have answered the Triple Bonus Question correctly! Your score of 1,280 is tripled, giving you a grand total of 3,840 points. As every other team lost all its points, DSA is the big winner of this year's All-Schools Brain-Power Tournament!"

Mordred and Brother Da~ feet, cheering and clapping. A few from the other schools clapped, too.

"The trophy!" cried Mordred, running up onto the stage. Tears of joy spilled down his cheeks. "Bring on the trophy! And don't forget to fill it with—" he consulted a parchment on which he had been taking notes, "—three thousand eight hundred forty golden coins!"

Now the red knight and the white knight appeared. They were pulling a cart that held a trophy the size of which Wiglaf had never seen. And spilling out of the enormous trophy were oodles and oodles of shiny gold coins.

"Oooooh!" cried Mordred when he saw the winnings. "Mine! All mine!" Then his violet eyes rolled up into his head, and the DSA headmaster fainted dead away. The red knight and the white knight grabbed him by the ankles. They dragged him off to the side of the stage.

Sir Verm stood beside the gold-filled trophy on the stage. He waited for the crowd to quiet down. "Thank you, ladies and gentlemen," Sir Verm said at last. "And thank you, Harkbert."

Harkbert bowed. Everyone clapped as the famous host flung his cape over one shoulder. They kept clapping as he bowed again and walked slowly off the stage.

"This has been a tournament to remember," said Sir Verm glumly. "For the first time ever, Knights Noble Conservatory lost. And I can tell you, it won't happen again. Er...I mean, it was an amazing upset."

Mordred groaned and sat up. "DSA won the tournament," he said as he got to his feet. He stumbled toward the trophy and threw his arms around it, crying, "Mine! All mine!"

Sir Verm stepped back from the gold-crazed headmaster.

"This solid-gold trophy will go home with the Dragon Slayers' Academy team for one year," Sir Verm continued.

"All mine," Mordred was muttering. "One... year?" He straightened up. "What are you talking about, one year?"

"This is a traveling trophy, sir," the KNC headmaster said. "You will have it in your DSA trophy case for a year. Then you must bring it back for next year's tournament."

Mordred's face fell. "Oh, woe!" he cried. "But...but...but the golden coins. They belong to me. All to me. Do they not?"

"That is correct," said Sir Verm. "All three thousand eight hundred and forty of them."

"Ah!" said Mordred. "That's not so bad then."

Sir Verm made a little speech then. He said it was probably good for KNC to lose once every hundred years. He said next year they'd be back on top again. There was one more round of applause. Then the fans stood up and filed out of the gym.

Brother Dave hurried up onto the stage. He hugged each member of the DSA team.

"I never doubted for a moment that thou wouldst win!" he told them.

Sir Verm turned to Mordred. "Take the cart, if you like," he offered. "You can bring the trophy back in it next year."

"All right," said Mordred. "Of course, next year is a long way away," he muttered. Then he picked a single gold coin out of the trophy. "Do not take this the wrong way, Sir Verm," he said. "But I always do this little test on my gold." So saying, he put the coin between his teeth and bit down, hard.

"EGAD!" he cried. "This coin! It is a fake!"

Wiglaf saw that the coin Mordred held between his thumb and forefinger was certainly not solid gold. A dark goo oozed out of it. Were the coins filled with some foul mold?

Once more the headmaster's violet eyes rolled up into his head. He collapsed onto the stage.

"Ake-fay?" Daisy exclaimed.

"He thought they were *solid* gold, did he?" asked Sir Verm. "Why, he never read the invitation to the tournament all the way through!" Then the KNC headmaster threw his head back and laughed long and loud.

Wiglaf picked a coin out of the trophy. He did not have much experience with gold. But this coin felt very light in his hand.

Erica did the same. "These coins are covered with gold-colored foil!" she exclaimed. She found a seam at the edge of a coin and picked at it with her fingernail. "And look! Inside the foil is..."

Angus put his nose down next to the coin and took a sniff.

"Chocolate!" he cried. He picked up a coin and quickly tore away the foil. He popped a circle of chocolate into his mouth. "Mmmmmm," he murmured as he closed his eyes and chewed. "Mmm."

"Of course it's chocolate," Sir Verm managed. "That's the prize for young scholars. That's what they want. Oh, to think that Mordred thought the coins were gold!"

"And a very fine grade of milk chocolate they are, too," Angus added, popping another one into his mouth. "Not too sweet. Not too bitter. Not one bit chalky."

Erica and Bragwort joined Angus in eating chocolate coins. Wiglaf peeled the foil off several pieces of chocolate and fed them to the DSA coach.

"Um-yay," said Daisy.

Then Wiglaf ate several himself.

Bragwort wiped his mouth on his sleeve, and said, "Who good."

"Bragwort!" Erica exclaimed. "Your spell is wearing off."

"Zelnoc's spells have a way of doing that," said Wiglaf.

Bragwort frowned. "Whoat spell? Whoat are you talking about?"

"Never mind, Bragwort," said Wiglaf. "Have some more chocolate. You, too, Brother Dave," he added.

"Well, maybe one," the monk said, taking a coin. "Because thou hast made me so proud! Ou-yay oo-tay, Aisy-day," he added. "Thou answered every question like the bright, eager pupils that thou art!"

"Thank you, Brother Dave," said Erica.

"You gave us our victory, Brother Dave," Wiglaf put in. "We won thanks to your words of wisdom about *if*."

Brother Dave beamed happily at his team. He reached for one more coin.

"There is just one thing that puzzles me," said Wiglaf.

"And what, pray tell, is that?" asked Brother Dave.

"Those questions about cabbage farming, washing dishes, and Sir Lancelot," said Wiglaf. "Why, it seemed almost as if those categories had been made for us."

Brother Dave smiled. "Who dost thou think made up the questions from DSA?" he asked.

"You?" said Wiglaf.

Brother Dave nodded. "And this morning, the knights just happened to pick three of my categories." He cast his eyes heavenward. "Miracles can happen! Never give up hope!"

Mordred stirred suddenly. He let out a pitiful moan.

Brother Dave quickly grabbed the cart handle.

"Here, lads," said the monk. "Takest thou this cart with thine trophy and thine coins. And runneth thou that a-way! Hurry! For thou dost not want to be here when Mordred waketh up."

"I'll say," said Angus. "For he shall surely gobble up a big part of the chocolate himself."

"Or he'll try to sell it at sky-high prices to the students back at DSA," added Erica.

"Then let us be off!" cried Wiglaf. He grabbed the cart handle and gave it a great yank. "If we beat Mordred back to DSA, we can share our winnings with our fellow students. Free chocolate for all!"

After a quick stop at Suite D to get their things, the team hurried across the KNC drawbridge and started back to DSA.

"I am the team captain," Bragwort said as they headed up the steep hill. "By rights, I should have the honor of pulling the cart to DSA."

"Certainly," said Erica.

"Absolutely," said Angus.

"If you insist," said Wiglaf.

Erica handed him the cart handle.

Bragwort took it. With a groan, he began pulling it up the hill.

Wiglaf smiled as they wended their way back home. They had made a proud name for DSA at the tournament. Their bellies were filled with something besides eel. And when they reached DSA with thousands of chocolate coins, they would surely be cheered as heroes.

~DSA~
YEARBOOK

Goldius est goodius!

The Campus of Dragon Slayers' Academy

DSA

Lady Lobelia's Chamber

Dr. Pluck's Science Lab

Tunnel Exit

Mordred's Classroom

Headmaster's Office

Stable

Castle Yard

Dining Hall

To Dungeon

Scrubbing Class

Practice Dragon

Yorick's Quick Change-O-Rama Camp Site

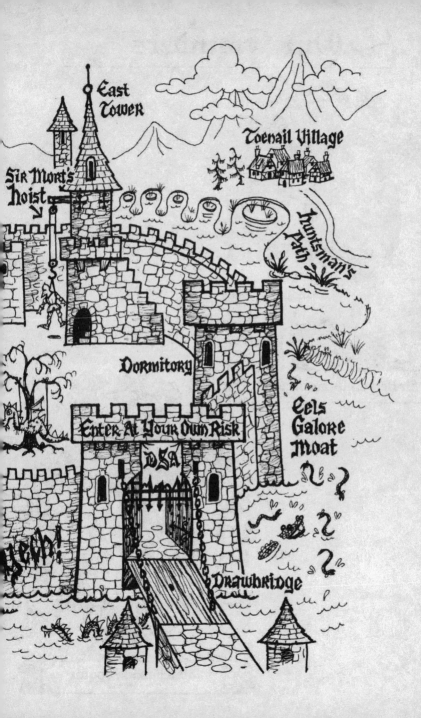

~Our Founders~

Sir Herbert Dungeonstone

Sir Ichabod Popquiz

～ Our Philosophy ～

Sir Herbert and Sir Ichabod founded
Dragon Slayers' Academy on a simple
principle still held dear today: Any lad—
no matter how weak, yellow-bellied, lazy,
pigeon-toed, smelly, or unwilling—can be
transformed into a fearless dragon slayer
who goes for the gold. After four years
at DSA, lads will finally be of some
worth to their parents, as well as a
source of great wealth to this distin-
guished academy.* ** ***

* Please note that Dragon Slayers' Academy is a strictly-for-profit
institution.

** Dragon Slayers' Academy reserves the right to keep some of the gold
and treasure that any student recovers from a dragon's lair.

*** The exact amount of treasure given to a student's family is deter-
mined solely by our esteemed headmaster, Mordred. The amount shall be
no less than 1/500th of the treasure and no greater than 1/499th.

～ Our Headmaster ～

Mordred de Marvelous

Mordred graduated from Dragon Bludgeon High, second in his class. The other student, Lionel Flyzwattar, went on to become headmaster of Dragon Stabbers' Prep. Mordred spent years as a part-time, semi-substitute student teacher at Dragon Whackers' Alternative School, all the while pursuing his passion for mud wrestling. Inspired by how filthy rich Flyzwattar had become by running a school, Mordred founded Dragon Slayers' Academy in CMLXXIV, and has served as headmaster ever since.

❧

Known to the Boys as: Mordred de Miser
Dream: Piles and piles of dragon gold
Reality: Yet to see a single gold coin
Best-Kept Secret: Mud wrestled under the name Macho-Man Mordie
Plans for the Future: Will retire to the Bahamas . . . as soon as he gets his hands on a hoard

Lady Lobelia

Lobelia de Marvelous is Mordred's sister and a graduate of the exclusive If-You-Can-Read-This-You-Can-Design-Clothes Fashion School. Lobelia has offered fashion advice to the likes of King Felix the Husky and Eric the Terrible Dresser. In CMLXXIX, Lobelia married the oldest living knight, Sir Jeffrey Scabpicker III. That's when she gained the title of Lady Lobelia, but—alas!—only a very small fortune, which she wiped out in a single wild shopping spree. Lady Lobelia has graced Dragon Slayers' Academy with many visits, and can be heard around campus saying, "Just because I live in the Middle Ages doesn't mean I have to look middle-aged."

Known to the Boys as: Lady Lo Lo
Dream: Frightfully fashionable
Reality: Frightful
Best-Kept Secret: Shops at Dark-Age Discount Dress Dungeon
Plans for the Future: New uniforms for the boys with mesh tights and lace tunics

Sir Mort du Mort

Sir Mort is our well-loved professor of Dragon Slaying for Beginners as well as Intermediate and Advanced Dragon Slaying. Sir Mort says that, in his youth, he was known as the Scourge of Dragons. (We're not sure what it means, but it sounds scary.) His last encounter was with the most dangerous dragon of them all: Knight-shredder. Early in the battle, Sir Mort took a nasty blow to his helmet and has never been the same since.

❧

Known to the Boys as: The Old Geezer
Dream: Outstanding Dragon Slayer
Reality: Just plain out of it
Best-Kept Secret: He can't remember
Plans for the Future: Taking a little nap

Coach Wendell Plungett

Coach Plungett spent many years questing in the Dark Forest before joining the Athletic Department at DSA. When at last he strode out of the forest, leaving his dragon-slaying days behind him, Coach Plungett was the most muscle-bulging, physically fit, manliest man to be found anywhere north of Nowhere Swamp. "I am what you call a hunk," the coach admits. At DSA, Plungett wears a number of hats—or, helmets. Besides PE Teacher, he is Slaying Coach, Square-Dance Director, Pep-Squad Sponsor, and Privy Inspector. He hopes to meet a damsel—she needn't be in distress—with whom he can share his love of heavy metal music and long dinners by candlelight.

❖

Known to the Boys as: Coach
Dream: Tough as nails
Reality: Sleeps with a stuffed dragon named Foofoo
Best-Kept Secret: Just pull his hair
Plans for the Future: Finding his lost lady love

Brother Dave

Brother Dave is the DSA librarian. He belongs to the Little Brothers of the Peanut Brittle, an order known for doing impossibly good deeds and cooking up endless batches of sweet peanut candy. How exactly did Brother Dave wind up at Dragon Slayers' Academy? After a batch of his extra-crunchy peanut brittle left three children from Toenail toothless, Brother Dave vowed to do a truly impossible good deed. Thus did he offer to be librarian at a school world-famous for considering reading and writing a complete and utter waste of time. Brother Dave hopes to change all that.

✤

Known to the Boys as: Bro Dave
Dream: Boys reading in the libary
Reality: Boys sleeping in the library
Best-Kept Secret: Uses Cliff's Notes
Plans for the Future: Copying out all the lyrics to "Found a Peanut" for the boys

Professor Prissius Pluck

Professor Pluck graduated
from Peter Piper Picked a
Peck of Pickled Peppers Prep,
and went on to become a
professor of Science at
Dragon Slayers' Academy.
His specialty is the Multiple
Choice Pop Test. The boys
who take Dragon Science,
Professor Pluck's popular
class,

a) are amazed at the great
quantities of saliva
Professor P. can project

b) try never to sit in the front row

c) beg Headmaster Mordred to transfer them to
another class

d) all of the above

⚜

Known to the Boys as: Old Spit Face

Dream: Proper pronunciation of *p*'s

Reality: Let us spray

Best-Kept Secret: Has never seen a pippi-hippo-
pappa-peepus up close

Plans for the Future: Is working on a cure for
chapped lips

Frypot

How Frypot came to be the cook at DSA is something of a mystery. Rumors abound. Some say that when Mordred bought the broken-down castle for his school, Frypot was already in the kitchen and he simply stayed on. Others say that Lady Lobelia hired Frypot because he was so speedy at washing dishes. Still others say Frypot knows many a dark secret that keeps him from losing his job. But no one ever, *ever* says that Frypot was hired because of his excellent cooking skills.

Known to the Boys as: Who needs a nickname with a real name like Frypot?
Dream: Cleaner kitchen
Reality: Kitchen cleaner
Best-Kept Secret: Takes long bubble baths in the moat
Plans for the Future: Has signed up for a beginning cooking class

Yorick

Yorick is Chief Scout at DSA.
His knack for masquerading as
almost anything comes from
his years with the Merry
Minstrels and Dancing
Damsels Players, where he
won an award for his role
as the Glass Slipper in
"Cinderella". However,
when he was passed over for
the part of Mama Bear in
"Goldilocks", Yorick decided
to seek a new way of life. He
snuck off in the night and, by
dawn, still dressed in the bear suit,
found himself walking up Huntsmans Path. Mordred
spied him from a castle window, recognized his talent
for disguise, and hired him as Chief Scout on the spot.

❖
Known to the Boys as: Who's that?
Dream: Master of Disguise
Reality: Mordred's Errand Boy
Best-Kept Secret: Likes dressing up as King Ken
Plans for the Future: To lose the bunny suit

Wiglaf of Pinwick

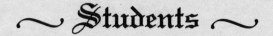

Wiglaf, our newest lad, hails from a hovel outside the village of Pinwick, which makes Toenail look like a thriving metropolis. Being one of thirteen children, Wiglaf had a taste of dorm life before coming to DSA and he fit right in. He started the year off with a bang when he took a stab at Coach Plungett's brown pageboy wig. Way to go, Wiggie! We hope to see more of this lad's wacky humor in the years to come.

❖

Dream: Bold Dragon-Slaying Hero
Reality: Still hangs on to a "security" rag
Extracurricular Activities: Animal-Lovers Club, President; No More Eel for Lunch Club, President; Frypot's Scrub Team, Brush Wielder; Pig Appreciation Club, Founder
Favorite Subject: Library
Oft-Heard Saying: *"Ello-hay, Aisy-day!"*
Plans for the Future: To go for the gold!

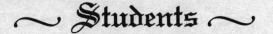

Angus du Pangus

The nephew of Mordred and Lady Lobelia, Angus walks the line between saying, "I'm just one of the lads" and "I'm going to tell my uncle!" Will this Class I lad ever become a mighty dragon slayer? Or will he take over the kitchen from Frypot some day? We of the DSA Yearbook staff are betting on choice #2. And hey, Angus? The sooner the better!

✦

Dream: A wider menu selection at DSA
Reality: Eel, Eel, Eel!
Extracurricular Activities: DSA Cooking Club, President; Smilin' Hal's Off-Campus Eatery, Sales Representative
Favorite Subject: Lunch
Oft-Heard Saying: *"I'm still hungry"*
Plans for the Future: To write *101 Ways to Cook a Dragon*

Eric von Royale

Eric hails from Someplace Far Away (at least that's what he wrote on his Application Form). There's an air of mystery about this Class I lad, who says he is "totally typical and absolutely average." If that is so, how did he come to own the rich tapestry that hangs over his cot? And are his parents really close personal friends of Sir Lancelot? Did Frypot the cook bribe him to start the Clean Plate Club? And doesn't Eric's arm ever get tired from raising his hand in class so often?

❖

Dream: Valiant Dragon Slayer
Reality: Teacher's Pet
Extracurricular Activities: Sir Lancelot Fan Club; Armor Polishing Club; Future Dragon Slayer of the Month Club; DSA Pep Squad, Founder and Cheer Composer
Favorite Subject: All of Them!!!!!
Oft-Heard Saying: *"When I am a mighty Dragon Slayer . . ."*
Plans for the Future: To take over DSA